EMERGENCY!

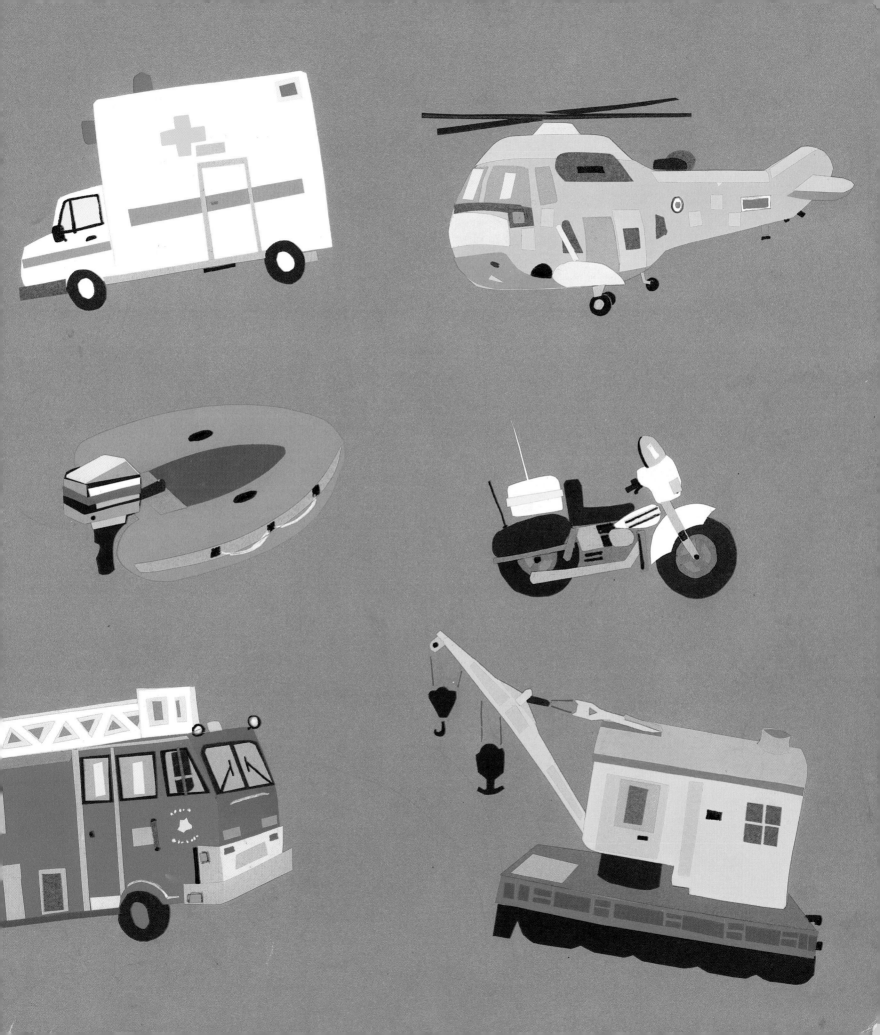

For Ann and Michael

MM

For Marcus, Michelle and Jay

AA

ORCHARD BOOKS
338 Euston Road, London NW1 3BH
Orchard Books Australia
Level 17/207 Kent Street, Sydney, NSW 2000
ISBN 978 1 84121 272 2
First published in 2002 by Orchard Books
First published in paperback in 2003
Text © Margaret Mayo 2002
Illustrations © Alex Ayliffe 2002
The rights of Margaret Mayo to be identified as the author and of Alex Ayliffe
to be identified as the illustrator of this work have been asserted by them
in accordance with the Copyrights, Designs and Patents Act, 1988.
A CIP catalogue record of this book is available from the British Library.
14
Printed in China
Orchard Books is a division of Hachette Children's Books,
an Hachette UK company.
www.hachette.co.uk

GENCY!

written
by
Margaret
Mayo

illustrated
by
Alex
Ayliffe

ORCHARD

Call 999 - emergency!
Burglars making a get-away!
Police car dashing, bright lights flashing;
Help is coming – it's on the way!

Ambulance speeding - **emergency!**
Whee-oww! Whee-oww! Pull over, make way!
Siren screaming, light beam-beaming;
Help is coming - it's on the way!

Tree on the track – **emergency!**
But breakdown train can clear the way,
Huge crane hooking,
lifting,
shifting;
Help is coming – it's on the way!

Boat sinking fast – emergency!
Launch a lifeboat in the storm and spray,
Long ropes tossing, lifebelt dropping;
Help is coming – it's on the way!

Vroom! Police motorbike - **emergency!**
Traffic build-up on the motorway.

Zipping, revving, cars directing;
Help is coming - it's on the way!

Forest fire blazing – emergency!
But fire-fighting planes zoom on their way,
swoop, swoop, swooping and water scooping;
Help is coming – it's on the way!

River flooding – emergency!
Inflatable boats needed – no delay,
Rescue supplies tugging, chug, chug, chugging;
Help is coming – it's on the way!

Big snowfall - **emergency!**
Snow plough slowly clears the way,
Pushing,
    shoving,
        tossing, tunnelling;
Help is coming - it's on the way!

Fire! Fire! – emergency!

Fire engines racing all the way,

Hoses slooshing,

water swooshing;

Help is coming –

it's on the way!

Man lost on mountain - **emergency!**
Helicopter hovering, whirr! whirr! hurray!

Searching, finding, winch door sliding;
Help is coming - it's on the way!

Quick! accident - emergency!
Damaged car is blocking the way.
Breakdown truck towing,
               yellow light glowing;
Help is coming - it's on the way!

All quiet now - no emergency,
No flashing, no dashing, no zooming away,
Resting and waiting for the next 999 call -
Then help will be coming, on its way!

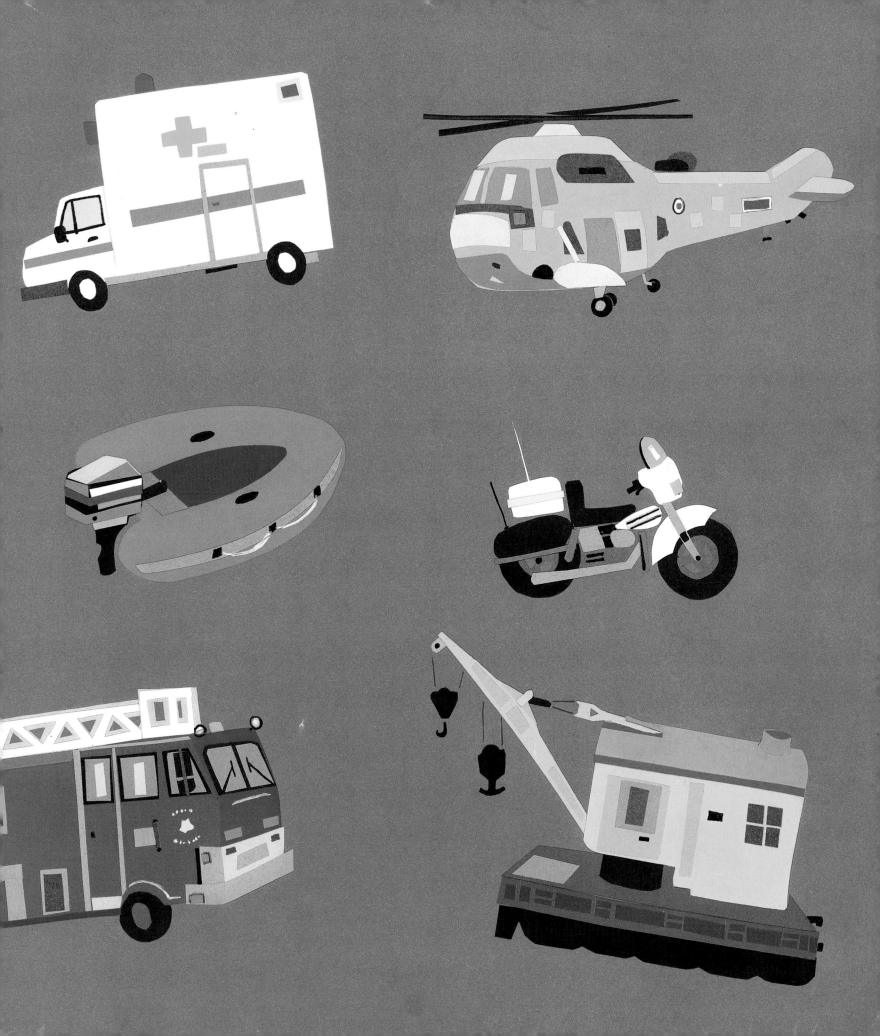

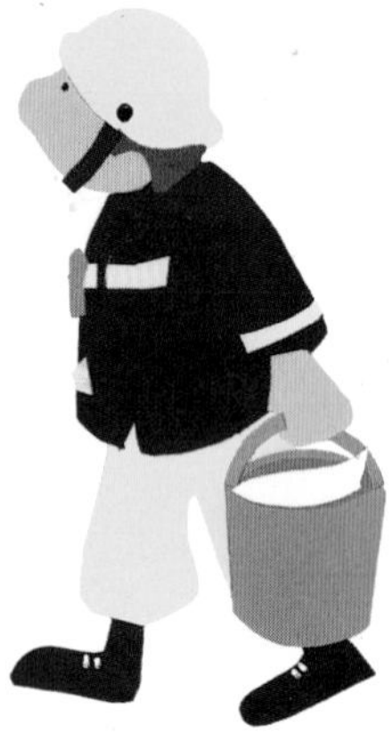